MARTHA SPEAKS™

Haunted House

Adaptation by Karen Barss
Based on a TV series teleplay written by Raye Lankford
Based on the characters created by Susan Meddaugh

HOUGHTON MIFFLIN HARCOURT
Boston • New York • 2010

Copyright © 2010 WGBH Educational Foun
"MARTHA" and all characters and underlying materials (including
copyright, trademarks, and registered trademarks of Susan
All other characters and materials are copyright a
All rights reserved. The PBS KIDS logo is a registered mark of

For information about permission to reproduce selections fro
Houghton Mifflin Harcourt Publishing Company, 215 Park Avenue   ...in 10003.

Green Light Readers and its logo are trademarks of Houghton Mifflin Harcourt Publishing Company.

Library of Congress Cataloging-in-Publication Data is on file.
ISBN 978-0-547-21073-5 pb | ISBN 978-0-547-39353-7 hc
Design by Rachel Newborn and Bill Smith Group
www.hmhbooks.com | www.marthathetalkingdog.com
Manufactured in China | LEO 10 9 8 7 6 5 4 3 2 1
4500230614

D1469283

Martha is helping at the flower shop.
"Can you deliver these flowers?"
Mom asks.
"Of course," Martha replies. "Where to?"

"This says nine thirty-six Elm Street, but nobody lives there." Mom frowns. "As kids, we thought that house was haunted!"

Mom smiles. "We were just being silly kids. Someone new must be moving in."

But Martha is worried.

Martha carries the basket.
She walks to the old house.
It looks eerie.
If I were a ghost, I would live here,
she thinks.

Inside, Mr. and Mrs. Parkington
are unpacking.
The furniture is covered in sheets.
The room is very dusty.

"I'm glad Great-Aunt Martha gave us this house," Mrs. Parkington says.
"But it *is* a little spooky. I'll feel better when the lights get turned on."

Martha scratches on the front door.
It slowly swings open. *Creeeaaakk!*
Inside it is dark and gloomy.

In the shadows, Martha runs
into something.
Martha jumps back and knocks
over a chair.
A sheet falls onto Martha.

Great ghostly granny!

Upstairs, Mrs. Parkington hears the
chair fall.
She gasps. "Is that a ghost?"
She tiptoes to the staircase.

"Who—who's there?" she calls downstairs.
Martha is also scared.
"It's muh-muh-muh-Martha," she says. "I
brought you some flowers."

Martha carries the basket across
the floor.
Mrs. Parkington does not know a dog is
under the sheet.
"Aaaaaah!" she screams. "A ghost!"

Mrs. Parkington drops her sheet.
It floats towards Martha.
"Aaaahh!" cries Martha. "A ghost!"

Martha runs all the way back to
the flower shop.
She tells Helen and T.D. about
the ghost.
"That is impossible," says Helen.

Then Mom says, "I'm sorry, Martha.
I gave you the wrong address.
Will you go and get the flowers back?"
Martha is scared.
Helen and T.D. offer to go back with her.

T.D., Martha, and Helen look at
the house.
"I told you it was spooky," Martha says.
"I am going in," says Helen, bravely.

She walks to the door and knocks.
The door swings open. *Creeeaaakk!*

Inside the dark hallway, Helen
hears footsteps!
She yelps and hides under
a sheet.

Outside, Martha hears Helen yelp.
Martha and T.D. try to open the door.
But it has closed and locked!

Helen runs to the back door.
She pulls at it.
"It's stuck!" she exclaims.

Martha and T.D. try to find another way in. They hear Helen call for help at the back door.
"We have to save Helen from the ghost!" says Martha.

Inside, the Parkingtons come across Helen.
They see her sheet and gasp.
They think *she* is a ghost!

Helen turns around and is happy to see
the Parkingtons.
"Oh, hello . . ." she says.
But they do not want to talk to a ghost.
They run away before Helen says
another word.

T.D. finally shoves open the back door.
"Where's the ghost?" he asks.
Helen laughs, "I guess *I* am the ghost!"

Can we leave now?